The Owl and the Tuba

Written by

James H. Lehman

Illustrated by

Christopher Raschka

Brotherstone Publishers
Elgin, Illinois

Published by
BROTHERSTONE PUBLISHERS
Elgin, IL 60123

Printed in the United States of America

Library of Congress Catalog Card Number: 91-73880

Lehman, James H.
The owl and the tuba/written by James H. Lehman;
illustrated by Christopher Raschka. p.   cm.
Summary: A fable about a tuba-playing boy who can't toot and
a wise old owl who can't hoot and how each finds his true but
unusual talent, much to the disgust of the squirrels.
ISBN 1-878925-02-4
[1. Owls – Fiction. 2. Animals – Fiction.
3. Musical Instruments – Fiction. 4. Occupations – Fiction.]
I. Raschka, Christopher, ill. II. Title.
PZ7.L   Ow 1991   [E]   91-73880

Once upon a time there was a boy named Fred who was learning to play the tuba.

Tubas
are loud,
rumbling
instruments
especially
when they
are played
by boys
who are just
learning,
and this
tuba and
this boy
were no
exception.
Fred
boomed
away on
his tuba
and nearly
drove his
parents
nuts.

Finally his mother couldn't stand it anymore and sent him out into the woods to practice.

And there he sat
every afternoon
on a stump under
an oak tree,
tooting away.

Fred thought
he was making
progress, but
everyone who
heard him
knew he wasn't.

The squirrels could testify
to that! They started stuffing acorns in
their ears. The truth of the matter was:
Fred couldn't toot worth a hoot.

Now it happened that
high in the oak tree lived
Hoomer the owl. Hoomer
was a wise old bird who
blinked his eyes
with great
dignity.

When a word
of wisdom was
needed, he would
take in a great
windy breath and
puff out his chest.
But when he released
all that air, no sound
came out of his beak.
The truth of
the matter was:
Hoomer the owl
couldn't hoot
worth a toot.

One day, to the great
relief of the squirrels,
Fred put his tuba down
on the stump, stretched
out on the grass, and
fell asleep. Hoomer had
been watching the boy
for some time and when
Fred started to snore,
Hoomer flew down to
check out the tuba.

He poked his
wise old head
into the bell.

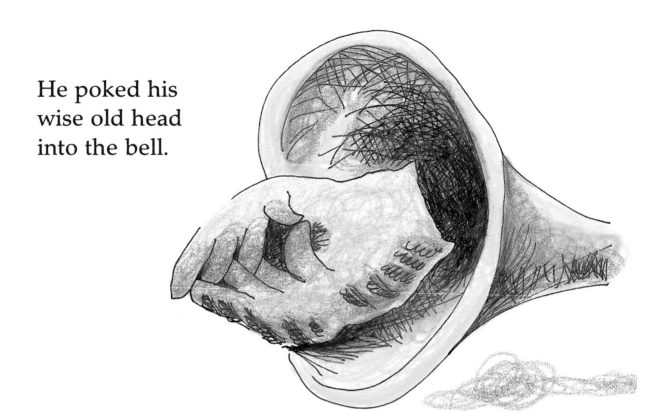

He flapped
his wings on
the valves.

He walked
carefully up
to the mouth-
piece, filled his
chest with one
of his great
windy breaths,
stuck his beak
in, and let go
a blast.

A mighty TOOT rumbled through the forest! Hoomer was so shocked he did a somersault and landed upside down in the bell. Fred woke up with a start; and four squirrels fell out of the oak tree.

That was the beginning of a great friendship. Every day Hoomer came down and perched on the bell of the tuba while Fred practiced. When he finished, Fred put the tuba on the stump and let Hoomer blow into it.

This went on day after day, and sad to say, the boy never got any better, but the owl was a born musician. By the end of the first week he was playing "Stars and Stripes Forever" and "Turkey in the Straw."

Sometimes while Hoomer was practicing,
Fred would wander through the woods,

and he noticed there were a lot of owls up in
the trees hooting back and forth to each other.

One day he let out a
hoot just for the fun
of it, and the whole
flock of owls flew
down and perched on
the limb above his
head, blinking at him.

He hooted
again and they
all nodded and
hooted back.
He tried out a
couple of other
hoots and soon
found with a
little trial and
error he could
speak their
language.

So every afternoon while Hoomer
tooted Fred hooted, and it wasn't
long until he could hoot better
than the owls themselves. Sometimes he would climb up on a limb
and tell them funny stories, and
they would sit there for hours,
blinking and nodding and shaking
with laughter.

Well, the friendship between Hoomer and Fred lasted for many years, and both the owl and the boy became famous. Hoomer taught the other owls to play trombone, trumpet, and piccolo and started the Hoomer Toots Brass Band and Piccolo Pipers. He toured the country and made an album.

Fred was so good at imitating birds that he went on to the university and became a great ornithologist.

And the squirrels? Well, they were disgusted by the whole thing and said it was weird, but there wasn't anything they could do about it.

Now there's a message in
this story. If you can't toot
worth a hoot, try hooting.
And if you can't hoot worth
a toot, try tooting...

. . . And you'll meet many squirrels who
will tell you it's weird, but don't pay
any attention to them.